Parents and Caregivers,

Stone Arch Readers are designed to provide enjoyable reading experiences, as well as opportunities to develop vocabulary, literacy skills, and comprehension. Here are a few ways to support your beginning reader:

- Talk with your child about the ideas addressed in the story.

- Discuss each illustration, mentioning the characters, where they are, and what they are doing.

- Read with expression, pointing to each word. You may want to read the whole story through and then revisit parts of the story to ensure that the meanings of words or phrases are understood.

- Talk about why the character did what he or she did and what your child would do in that situation.

- Help your child connect with characters and events in the story.

Remember, reading with your child should be fun, not forced. Each moment spent reading with your child is a priceless investment in his or her literacy life.

Gail Saunders-Smith, Ph.D.

STONE ARCH READERS
are published by Stone Arch Books, a Capstone Imprint
1710 Roe Crest Drive
North Mankato, Minnesota 56003
www.capstonepub.com

Klein, Adria F. (Adria Fay), 1947–

City Train in trouble / by Adria Klein ;
illustrated by Craig Cameron.
p. cm. -- (Stone Arch readers: Train time)
Summary: City Train needs a little help to get started.
ISBN 978-1-4342-4783-4 (library binding)
ISBN 978-1-4342-6196-0 (pbk.)
1. Locomotives--Juvenile fiction. 2. Railroad trains--
Juvenile fiction. [1. Locomotives--Fiction. 2. Railroad trains--
Fiction.] I. Cameron, Craig, ill. II. Title.
PZ7.K678324Cji 2013
[E]--dc23   2012046959

Reading Consultants:
Gail Saunders-Smith, Ph.D.
Melinda Melton Crow, M.Ed.
Laurie K. Holland, Media Specialist
Designer: Russell Griesmer

Printed in the united States of America
10872R

City Train in Trouble

written by
Adria F. Klein

illustrated by
Craig Cameron

STONE ARCH BOOKS
a capstone imprint

"I am done. Time to go home,"
City Train said.

She tooted her horn.

The people waved good-bye.

But City Train did not move.

She tooted her horn again.

The people waved good-bye again.

But City Train did not move.

"I am stuck," City Train said.

"We can help," the people said.

The people pushed City Train.

She started to move.

The people waved good-bye.

"Thank you!" City Train said.

Toot! Toot!

STORY WORDS

tooted   good-bye   pushed

waved   stuck   started

Word Count: 72

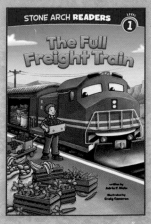